Stephen B. Weeks

The University of North Carolina in the Civil War

an address delivered at the centennial celebration of the opening of the

institution, June 5th, 1895

Stephen B. Weeks

The University of North Carolina in the Civil War
an address delivered at the centennial celebration of the opening of the institution,
June 5th, 1895

ISBN/EAN: 9783337223274

Printed in Europe, USA, Canada, Australia, Japan

Cover: Foto ©Andreas Hilbeck / pixelio.de

More available books at **www.hansebooks.com**

"The University of North Carolina in the Civil War."

AN ADDRESS

DELIVERED AT THE

CENTENNIAL CELEBRATION

OF THE

OPENING OF THE INSTITUTION,

JUNE 5TH, 1895,

BY

STEPHEN BEAUREGARD WEEKS, Ph. D.

REPRINTED FROM THE SOUTHERN HISTORICAL SOCIETY PAPERS,
VOLUME XXIV.

RICHMOND:
WM. ELLIS JONES, STEAM BOOK AND JOB PRINTER.
1896.

"The University of North Carolina in the Civil War."

AN ADDRESS

Delivered at the Centennial Celebration of the Opening of the Institution, June 5th, 1895.

By Stephen Beauregard Weeks, Ph. D.

I. General Introduction.

"First at Bethel; last at Appomattox." Such is the laconic inscription on the new monument to the Confederate dead which was recently unveiled in Raleigh. There is an especial appropriateness in the erection of this monument by the people of North Carolina in their organic capacity, for these men died at the command of their State, and it was exceedingly proper that she should thus honor them.

The heroic in history but seldom occurs. It is not often that the life of nations rises above the monotonous level which characterizes the daily routine of duty. When such periods do occur they are usually as a part of some great national uprising like the *levé en masse* in France under the first Napoleon, or the Landsturm in Germany in 1813. Of the American States, none can show a fairer record in this respect than North Carolina. There is little in the Colonial or State history of North Carolina that is discreditable. The key-note to the whole of her Colonial history is unending opposition to unjust and illegal government, by whom or whenever exercised. Before the colony was well in its teens it had expelled one of its governors from office, and a better man, one who was more in sympathy with the people, had taken his place; and before the colony was thirty, another governor, although one of the Lords Proprietors had been impeached, deprived of his office, and expelled the province. It was this fearlessness in what they conceived to be their rights that carried her people through the troublous period of the "Cary Rebellion," so called; enabled them to meet with a firm hand the brow-beating and the villainies, as well as the flattery, of proprietary and royal governors and put them among the leaders in the movement that culminated in the Revolution.

Then came a time of peace and calm when the people pursued the even tenor of their way, and sought in field and forum to find solution for the problems amid which their lot was cast. This period lasted for about two generations, and during it the University of North Carolina had been founded and was seeking a greater expansion. During the period from the end of the Revolution to the Civil War there are no mountain peaks in her history; the level of uniformity is hardly broken by a single event of importance, and there is little in it to attract the attention of the student of the philosophy of history. But there is a period in the history of North Carolina which stands pre-eminent. There is a time which deserves to be characterized as the HEROIC PEROID of the State. This is the period of the Civil War and Reconstruction. Let all other parts of our history be forgotten, this period of itself, though it be less than half a generation in all, will place North Carolina among the heroic in history.

During those terrible years we see a renaissance of the ideas which characterized pre-eminently the men of the Colonial period. The men of '61 showed that the spirit of Colonial North Carolina was still abroad in the land, and their watchword became again resistance to what they believed to be unjust government, and with this as a basis they conducted a struggle for success that has few parallels in history. They sought to carry out again the program of their colonial ancestors, even to the impeachment and deposition of their governor.

In the movement which led up to the war North Carolina took the part of a conservative, ambitious for peace. She sought to escape the necessity of war by all the means in her power; but, when the die was cast and war was no longer avoidable, she entered into the struggle with characteristic energy, and prosecuted it to the end, and when the end came, no State accepted the crushing defeat with more steadfast loyalty than North Carolina, or sought with more energy to build up the waste places. Then came what was worse than defeat, "impartial suffrage," which meant disfranchisement of whites and enfranchisement of blacks, then the terrors of reconstruction and negro rule broke over us like the roar of some terrible simoon, bearing in its path further humiliation, accompanied by a corrupt government, increased taxes, and a depreciation of values.

Such was the struggle through which the best men of North Carolina were called to pass in those fateful years between 1860 and 1875. These were the years on which the fate of the future in a large measure depended. Well did the brave men of that generation come to the succor of the foundering ship of State, and nobly did they rescue her from the rule of her motley crew. The best men of North Carolina were engaged in this work, and among them, most frequently as leaders, were many alumni of the University of North Carolina.

II. University Men in Public Life.

Before beginning to trace the career of the alumni of the University of North Carolina in the Civil War, it will be of interest for us to review briefly the influence of that institution on the nation as a whole. Before 1861 the University of North Carolina had furnished one President of the United States, James K. Polk; one Vice President, William R. King; two Presidents of the United States Senate, Willie P. Mangum and William R. King; seven Cabinet officers, John H. Eaton, (War), John Branch (Navy), John Y. Mason (Navy and Attorney General), William A. Graham (Navy), James C. Dobbin (Navy), Jacob Thompson (Interior), and Aaron V. Brown (P. M. G.) She had had two foreign ministers of the first rank, William R. King and John Y. Mason; (both to France), and three of the second rank, Daniel M. Barringer, John H. Eaton and Romulus M. Saunders, (all to Spain). She had furnished three Governors to Florida, John Branch, (Ter.), John H. Eaton, (Ter.), and W. D. Moseley; two to Tennessee, A. O. P. Nicholson and James K. Polk; and one to New Mexico, Abram Rencher. Of United States Senators, she had had Branch, Brown, Graham, Haywood and Mangum of North Carolina; A. O. P. Nicholson of Tennessee; Thomas H. Benton of Missouri, and William R. King of Alabama. Benton served for thirty years in succession; King served twenty-nine years in all, and these two records are still among the first in point of service. The University had furnished forty-one members of the House of Representatives, and included in the number James K. Polk as speaker. She had given two justices to the Supreme Court of North Carolina; two Chancellors to Tennessee; a Chief Justice to Florida; a Chief Justice to Alabama, and five bishops to the Protestant Episcopal church (Davis, Green, C. S. Hawks, Otey, Polk); besides a number of college presidents, professors in colleges and leaders in other walks of life.

III. The Position of the University in North Carolina in 1861.

When we come to study the influence of this University on North Carolina itself, it will be seen that that influence was all powerful. The first alumnus to attain the Governor's chair was William Miller in 1814. Between this date and the deposition of Governor Vance in 1866, no less than fourteen out of twenty governors were University men—Miller, Branch, Burton, Owen, Swain, Spaight, Morehead, Graham, Manly, Winslow, Bragg, Ellis, Clark, and Vance. They filled the chair thirty-eight years out of the fifty-two. The influence of the University was not less paramount in North Carolina at the outbreak of the war in 1861 than it had been in former years. The governor in 1861, John W. Ellis, and his opponent on the Whig ticket in 1860, John Pool, were both alumni. The two Senators in Congress in 1861, Thomas Bragg and Thomas L. Clingman; four of the Representatives in Congress, L. O'B. Branch, Thomas Ruffin, Z. B. Vance, and Warren Winslow, were University men. The speakership of the State Senate, under Warren Winslow, W. W. Avery, Henry T. Clark, Giles Mebane, M. E. Manly, and Tod R. Caldwell, was constantly under the direction of University men between 1854 and 1870. With the exception of a period of fifteen years, this office was continuously in the hands of University men between 1815 and 1870. Thomas Settle was Speaker of the House of Commons in 1858, 1859, and 1863; R. B. Gilliam in 1862; R. S. Donnell in 1864; and with the exception of twenty years they had filled the office continuously since 1812. The members of the Supreme Court of the State, M. E. Manly, W. H. Battle, and R. M. Pearson, were all alumni. Of the judges of the Superior Court in 1861, the University was represented by John L. Bailey, Romulus M. Saunders, James W. Osborne, George Howard, Jr., and Thomas Ruffin, Jr. In the same way four of the solicitors were University men, Elias C. Hines, Thomas Settle, Jr., Robert Strange, and David Coleman, and William A. Jenkins, the Attorney-General (1856–62), made a fifth. All of his predecessors in the office of Attorney-General since 1810 had been University men, except those filling the position for a period of fourteen years. Daniel W. Courts, State Treasurer (1852–63), was another alumnus, and so had been his predecessors since 1837, except for two years. Three of the successful Breckinridge electors in 1860, John W. Moore, A. M. Scales, and William B. Rodman, were alumni. This list of the public officials will show conclusively that the large majority of the more important positions in the State were filled by the alumni of the University. They were the men who controlled the destinies of the State in 1861.

IV. Union Sentiment in North Carolina in 1861.

North Carolina was the last to enter the Confederacy, and her slowness was due, beyond question, to the paramount influence exercised by the conservative views of the alumni of the University. Willie P. Mangum, who had been the personal friend of the abolition Senator, William H. Seward, when the latter first entered the United States Senate, had said in the Senate long before, when the nullification of South Carolina was the topic of the day: "If I could coin my heart into gold, and it were lawful in the sight of Heaven, I would pray God to give me firmness to do it, to save the Union from the fearful, the dreadful shock which I verily believe impends." His feelings were not changed by time, and in 1860 he said to his nephew who had been taught in the school of Calhoun and Yancey, and now talked loudly of secession, that if he were an emperor the nephew should be hanged for treason. The Union sentiments of Governor Graham, Governor Morehead, of Governor Vance, and General Barringer, were just as pronounced as were those of Judge Mangum. All of the old line Whigs opposed the war, while some of the Democrats, like Bedford Brown, denied the right to secede.

V. Action of North Carolina Assembly, 1860-'61.

With such sentiments as these from her leading men it is hardly a matter of surprise that North Carolina moved slowly in the consideration of this great question. On the other hand, Judge S. J. Person, the leader of the secession forces in North Carolina, was also a University man, and on December 10th, 1860, as Chairman of the Committee on Federal Relations, made a report to the General Assembly, in which it was recommended that a convention be elected on February 7th, 1861, to meet on the 18th, to consider the grave situation. A minority report was signed by three members of the committee, Giles Mebane, Col. David Outlaw, and Nathan Newby, all University men, in which they opposed the calling of a convention, on the ground that it was "premature and unnecessary." The conservatives carried their point and no convention was called.

During the month of January, 1861, various delegations were received from the more southern States which had already seceded. It was the duty of these commissioners to bring North Carolina over, if possible, to the side of the Confederacy. The University found three of her alumni among these commissioners: Isham W. Garrott, from Alabama; Jacob Thompson, from Mississippi, and Samuel Hall, from Georgia. The Assembly of North Carolina had also received an invitation from the State of Alabama to send a delegation to meet similar delegations from other States at Montgomery in February, 1861. The State sent a committee "for the purpose of effecting an honorable and amicable adjustment of all the difficulties which distract the country, upon the basis of the Crittenden resolutions," and the parties chosen were all University men: President D. L. Swain, General M. W. Ransom, and Colonel John L. Bridgers. In the same way three of the five commissioners sent by North Carolina to attend the Peace Congress in Washington in 1861 were University men. They were J. M. Morehead, George Davis, and D. M. Barringer.

Finally, on January 30th, 1861, through the strenuous efforts of Judge S. J. Person, W. W. Avery, and Victor C. Barringer, all again University men, the Assembly of North Carolina passed an act providing for the calling of a convention. The election was on the 28th of February. In Holden's paper, *The Standard*, of the 20th of March, the official figures are given as 467 against a convention.* The same paper estimates that out of 93,000 votes cast at this election, 60,000 were in favor of the Union, and that 20,000 sympathizers with the same side staid from the polls. Of the delegates elected about eighty-three were for the Union, and only about thirty-seven for secession. Some of the counties, like Caswell, voted against the convention, but chose Union delegates; others, like Wake, voted for convention and chose Union delegates. In Raleigh the vote was nearly nine to one in favor of the Union. No convention was therefore called and secession was defeated for the second time in North Carolina.

But all the efforts towards a peaceful solution of the problem were failures; Sumpter was fired on and President Lincoln issued his call for 75,000 troops. The share of North Carolina was two regiments.

---

* Add to this 194 majority from Davie, which arrived too late to be put into the official returns, and we find a majority of 661 against a convention.

The reply of Governor Ellis to this call for troops, addressed to Hon. Simon Cameron, Secretary of War, on the 15th of April, marked him as a man of prompt decision and great force of character. It was to be for four long years the watch word of a great State and was but the chrystalized sentiment of the people of that day: "Your dispatch is received, and if genuine, which its extraordinary character leads me to doubt, I have to say in reply that I regard the levy of troops made by the administration for the purpose of subjugating the States of the South as in violation of the Constitution, and a gross usurpation of power. I can be no party to this wicked violation of the laws of the country, and to this war upon the liberties of a free people. You can get no troops from North Carolina."

VI. THE NORTH CAROLINA SECESSION CONVENTION.

The next and the inevitable step was the Convention of 1861. It was provided for by act of May 1; the election was held May 13; on the 20th the Convention met; on the same day, North Carolina, after much deliberation, after a long consideration which might have been termed cowardice by more hotheaded neighbors, passed the ordinance of secession. She had been the last of the Southern States to enter the Federal union; she was the last to sever her connection with it. In this convention, as elsewhere, University of North Carolina men were all powerful. The following were her contribution to the Convention of 1861:

Alexander county, A. C. Stewart; Beaufort, R. S. Donnell; Bladen, Thomas D. McDowell; Brunswick, Thomas D. Meares; Caldwell, Edmund W. Jones (?); Camden, Dennis D. Ferebee; Carteret, Charles R. Thomas; Caswell, Bedford Brown; Chatham, J. H. Headen, John Manning, L. J. Merritt; Cumberland, Warren Winslow, Malcolm J. McDuffie (?); Davidson, B. A. Kittrell; Duplin, Joseph T. Rhodes; Edgecombe, William S. Battle, George Howard, Jr.; Forsyth, Rufus L. Patterson; Gaston, Sidney X. Johnston; Guilford, John A. Gilmer, R. P. Dick; Halifax, Richard H. Smith; Henderson, William M. Shipp; Iredell, Anderson Mitchell; Mecklenburg, William Johnston, James W. Osborne; New Hanover, R. H. Cowan. Robert Strange; Northampton, D. A. Barnes; Orange, William A. Graham; Perquimans, Joseph S. Cannon (?); Person, John W. Cunningham; Pitt, Bryan Grimes; Randolph, William J. Long, Alfred

G. Foster; Richmond, Walter F. Leak; Rowan, Burton Craige, Hamilton C. Jones, Richard A. Caldwell; Sampson, Thomas Bunting (?); Stokes, John Hill; Wake, Kemp P. Battle; Washington, William S. Pettigrew; Wayne, George V. Strong.

The Convention had 120 members. Resignations, deaths, and new elections increased this number to about 139. About one-third of these had been students in this University. The secretaryship of the convention was given to one of her sons, Colonel Walter L. Steele, the assistant secretaryship to another, Leonidas C. Edwards, and she had more than her share of the ability of the convention. After we except the names of Judge Badger, Judge Ruffin, Judge Biggs, W. W. Holden, Kenneth Rayner, Governor Reid, E. J. Warren, and a few others, it will be seen that most of the leaders were University men.

When the convention came, on the 18th of June, to choose Senators and Representatives from North Carolina to the Provisional Congress of the Confederate States, which met in Richmond, in July 1861, the dominating influence of the University was still more powerfully felt. Four men were nominated for the senatorships: George Davis, W. W. Avery, Bedford Brown and Henry W. Miller. They were all University men. Seven others received votes without a formal nomination; five of these, W. A. Graham, Thomas Bragg, William Eaton, Jr., John M. Morehead, and George Howard, Jr., were University men. Davis and Avery were chosen. For the eight seats in the Confederate House of Representatives, 17 candidates were presented. Eight candidates were University men and four of these were elected: Burton Craige, Thomas D. McDowell, John M. Morehead and Thomas Ruffin, Jr. As Judge Waller R. Staples, of Virginia, was also a member, the University of North Carolina had seven alumni as delegates to this session of the Provisional Congress. When we come to the two Congresses of the Confederate States, we find that the University had two representatives in the Senate, George Davis (1), and William A. Graham (2), while Thomas S. Ashe was chosen for the third which never met. In the House she had David W. Lewis, of Georigia (1); Thomas S. Ashe (1), R. R. Bridgers (1), Thomas C. Fuller (2), John A. Gilmer (2), Thomas D. McDowell (1), and Josiah Turner (2), of North Carolina; and Waller R. Staples, of Virginia.

VII. ALUMNI IN CONFEDERATE EXECUTIVE SERVICE.

Some of her alumni were in the executive service. John Manning was a receiver of the Confederate States. Jacob Thompson was confidential agent to Canada. His object was to open communications with secret organizations of anti-war men in Ohio, Indiana and Illinois, to arrange for their organization and arming so that they, when strong enough, might demand a cessation of hostilities on the part of the Federal government. Thompson was of much service also in collecting and forwarding supplies, conducting communications with the outside world, &c. He acquired no little notoriety in connection with the attempted release of Confederate prisioners from Rock Island, Camp Chase and Chicago; suffered the unjust accusation of sending infected clothing into the union lines from Canada, and came perilously near having the distinction conferred upon him of being made the scape goat to bear the infamy of the assassination of Lincoln.

Two sons of the University served as the head of the Confederate Department of Justice. Thomas Bragg was the second and George Davis the fourth Attorney General.

Other alumni served their individual States in various civil ways. The three commissioners of the North Carolina Board of Claims elected in 1861 were all University men, B. F. Moore, S. F. Phillips, and P. H. Winston. When an agent was appointed later in the war to audit the financial dealings of the State with the Confederacy, P. H. Winston, the third member of the Board of Claims, was chosen for that responsible position. George V. Strong became Confederate District Attorney for North Carolina in 1862; Robert B. Gilliam and William M. Shipp became judges of the superior court in North Carolina in 1862 and 1863 respectively. Thomas C. Manning was chairman of the commission appointed by the governor of Louisiana to investigate the outrages committed by Federal troops under Gen. Banks during the invasion of Western Louisiana in 1863 and 1864. Manning and H. M. Polk were members of the Louisiana secession convention of 1861, and John T. Wheat was its secretary. John Bragg was a member of the Alabama, and A. H. Carrigan of the Arkansas convention and Arthur F. Hopkins was sent by the governor of Alabama as special agent to Virginia. Were it possible for us to obtain the complete history of each one of our students in the more Southern States, it would no doubt be found to be a fact that our alumni, where ever they were, held more than their proportionate share of the places of trust and honor and of the posts of danger.

VIII. University Men in Military Service.

The above summary has given us a survey of the civil service rendered during the war by the alumni of the University of North Carolina. We have noted how completely they dominated the control of the State in 1861. We have seen that the representatives of the University of North Carolina in the Confederate Congress was fair, but not extraordinarily large. We now come to the officers in the field.

The highest military rank held by a University man was that of Lieutenant-General. This was attained by Leonidas Polk under a commission dated Oct. 10, 1862. Gen. Polk was outranked in length of service only by Longstreet and Kirby-Smith. He had been made Major-General on June 25, 1861; he was the second person to attain this rank, and, of the 99 Major Generals in the service, was, with one exception, the only man to attain this position without passing through the preliminary grade of Brigadier.

The University had one other son to attain the rank of Major General, Bryan Grimes, commissioned Feb. 23, 1865.

Of Brigadier Generals she had thirteen.

George Burgwyn Anderson, commissioned, June 9, 1862.
Rufus Barringer, commissioned June 1, 1864.
Lawrence O'Bryan Branch, commissioned, Nov. 16, 1861.
Thomas Lanier Clingman, commissioned May 17, 1862.
Isham W. Garrott, commissioned May 28, 1863.
Richard Caswell Gatlin, commissioned July 8, 1861.
Bryan Grimes, commissioned May 19, 1864.
Robert Daniel Johnston, commissioned Sept. 1, 1863.
William Gaston Lewis, commissioned May 31, 1864.
James Johnston Pettigrew, commissioned Feb. 26, 1862.
Chas. W. Phifer, commissioned spring of 1862.
Matt Whitaker Ransom commissioned June 13, 1863.
Alfred Moore Scales, commissioned June 13, 1863.

Among the staff appointments we find that the third Adjutant and Inspector General, R. C. Gatlin, was a son of this University. He was commissioned August 26, 1863, and in July 1862, had been made a Major-General of N. C. S. T. The first assistant Adjutant General, was J. F. Hoke (1861); the first Quartermaster General was L. O'B. Branch; the first Commissary General was Col. William Johnston. Matt. W. Ransom was made a Major-General in 1865 and Col. John D. Barry was commissioned a Brigadier-General, with temporary rank, on the third of August, 1864.

In the medical department we find Dr. Peter E. Hines as the Medical Director of North Carolina troops, Dr. E. Burke Haywood as surgeon of the General Hospital at Raleigh, and Joseph H. Baker was the first assistant Surgeon of North Carolina troops, commissioned in 1861. Other alumni rendered similar services to other states; Ashley W. Spaight was Brigadier-General in the service of Texas; Thomas C. Manning was Adjutant-General of Louisana in 1863, with the rank of Brigadier; Jacob Thompson was an Inspector-General.

Should full information ever be obtained it will no doubt appear that there were other cases where alumni of this University served their States in high military capacity, although not forming a part of the regular army of the Confederate States.

When we come to the list of colonels and lieutenant-colonels their number is very large. These were furnished to the Confederacy by North Carolina: seventy-six regiments (besides thirteen battalions and a few other troops, making, perhaps, in all eighty full regiments). Out of the seventy-six regular regiments we find that forty-eight had at one time or another a son of this University in the first or second place of command. The list includes forty-five colonels and twenty-nine lieutenant-colonels. We are to remember also that all of the alumni of the institution did not serve with the North Carolina troops, and we must keep their record also in view. From the best sources obtainable, the catalogues of the Philanthropic and Dialectic Societies, it seems that not less than sixty-three Alumni attained the rank of colonel in the various regiments furnished by the different States to the Confederacy, and that not less than thirty became lieutenant-colonels.

IX. THE ALUMNI IN BATTLE.

Having taken this general survey of the power and influence wielded by University men in public affairs in 1860-'61, and of the higher positions in the army of the Confederate States filled by them, it now becomes our duty to review the humbler, but no less important positions in the service which were filled by her alumni; to trace the rising spirit of enthusiasm among her students in 1861; to follow their fortunes in the dark and evil days, and then to tell the story of her experience during the closing days of the struggle.

To come then, first of all, to the "spirit of '61." When the war began the boys of the University rushed away to the struggle like men who had been bidden to a marriage feast. There was great vivacity of spirit, even gaiety of temper displayed, and Governor Swain was proud of their enthusiasm. But enthusiasm was not confined to the University. The residents of the village of Chapel Hill were among the earliest to enter the service. They had their representatives at Bethel. A company was organized early in April. Among its officers were R. J. Ashe, as captain; R. B. Saunders and R. Mallett, as second lieutenants, and Thomas G. Skinner, as fourth corporal. It will thus be seen that the company was under the direction of University men. There were other University men among the privates: F. A. Fetter, a tutor, was there to represent the faculty; J. R. Hogan, A. J. McDade, J. H. McDade, Lewis Maverick, Spier Whitaker, Jr., represented the student body and the alumni. There were others not associated with the University, but who have helped to make Chapel Hill and its vicinity honored and respected. Their names will be recognized: J. F. Freeland, Jones Watson, E. W. Atwater, J. W. Atwater, Baxter King, W. N. Mickle, D. McCauley, S. F. Patterson, and W. F. Stroud, at present M. C., from the Fourth North Carolina District. This organization was known as the Orange Light Infantry, and became Company D of the First North Carolina, or Bethel Regiment, so called because of its participation in the battle of Bethel. The regiment had been enlisted for six months, and after its term of service expired, was disbanded. The Orange Light Infantry then broke up, and its members attached themselves to other commands. Four companies were raised in Chapel Hill and vicinity during the war. Governor Swain is responsible for the statement that thirty of these volunteers fell in battle or died in hospitals. Company G, Eleventh North Carolina, was one of those companies that was made up with volunteers from Chapel Hill and the surrounding sections of Orange, with a few from Chatham county.

The following members of this company (G) lost their lives:

KILLED IN BATTLE.

First Lieutanant John H. McDade, July 1, 1863; Second Lieutenant James W. Williams, July 1, 1863; Second Lieutanant N. B. Tenny, July 1, 1863; Corporals W. S. Durham, W. G. Ivey, J. J. Snipes, July 1, 1863, Lueco Ferrell, Oct. 27, 1864; Privates Wesley Andrews, Cornelius Edwards, William Pendergrass, Esau Garrett, July 1, 1863, T. J. Whittaker, Aug. 21, 1864, W. D. Flintoff, Oct. 1, 1864.

DIED OF DISEASE.

Captain J. R. Jennings, of yellow fever, Sept. 10, 1862; Privates H. T. Burgess, George Cole, Carney Haitchcock, Whitfield King, July, 1862; John W. Lloyd, Forest Pearson, Edward Pearson, April, 1862; William Potts, April, 1863; James K. Gaths, of small pox, Feb. 1864; W. B. Cates, William Cates, Feb. 1863; Anderson Turner, May 25, 1863; William Petty, Nov. 26, 1863; Corporal D. J. Norwood, Sept. 1863; Private J. M. Pendergrass, Oct. 1864; Forrest Williams, Nov. 1864; John W. Craig, Feb. 1865; John W. Potts, July, 1865; Edward Reaves, 1864; Ruffin Allen, Oct. 1864; William Jolly, Nov, 1864.

Our University cannot claim all of these as her sons. But their distinguished bravery ranks them among their comrades who had been more fortunate in educational advantages. We know also that a number of residents of Chapel Hill and its vicinity, who belonged to other commands, lost their lives in the service. Their names are as follows:

Maj. John H. Whitaker, Capt. Elijah G. Morrow, Capt. William Stone, Lieutenants Wesley Lewis Battle, Richardson Mallett, William N. Mickle; Sergeant Thomas L. Watson; Privates, Alex. R. Morrow, William Baldwin, Junius C. Battle, Willis Nunn, Henry Roberson; Sergeant-major Edward Jones.

If we credit the above list, whom we know to have been residents of Chapel Hill, and the members of Company G., 11th North Carolina, who lost their lives, to Chapel Hill, it will be seen that this small village and vicinity contributed no less than forty-nine of its sons to the cause of the Confederacy.

Nor was enthusiasm and devotion to the call of duty confined to the village of Chapel Hill or to the students and alumni of the

University of North Carolina. The University faculty was not slower than the student body. Five of them volunteered for the war. The other nine, with one exception, were either clergymen or beyond age. Of the members who volunteered, William J. Martin, the professor of chemistry, was made major of the 11th North Carolina; was promoted lieutenant-colonel and colonel of the same; fought bravely through the war; was wounded at Bristow Station and surrendered at Appomattox. There were for the year 1860–61 five tutors in the University. All of them volunteered. Four of them fell in the service. F. A. Fetter was with the Bethel regiment as we have already seen. He alone of the five survived. The first of these tutors to seal his faith with his blood was Captain George Burgwyn Johnston, who died in Chapel Hill in 1863, of a decline brought on by prison hardships at Sandusky, Ohio. The next was Lieutenant Iowa Michigan Royster, who fell with the song of Dixie on his lips, while leading his company to the charge at Gettysburg. He was one of 8 in the class of 1860 who received first distinction; within four years, four of these filled soldiers' graves. Another of these first honor men, and the youngest, was Captain George Pettigrew Bryan. He was to have entered the ministry; but his country called and he surrendered his young life at Charles City Road, in 1864. His promotion as Lieutenant-Colonel, arrived just after his death. The fourth tutor to fall was Robert W. Anderson who had been a candidate for orders in the Episcopal Church. He was a brother of General George Burgwyn Anderson and like him offered his sword and his life to his State   He fell at the Wilderness in 1864.

Such was the contribution of the faculty of the University of North Carolinia to the fighting forces of the Confederacy. It contributed six volunteers; four were slain. We must add to this list the names of several others who had been in former years connected with the University in the capacity of tutors. Of the career of Jacob Thompson we have already spoken. We know also the military record of eight others at least: R. H. Battle, W. R. Wetmore, P. E. Spruill, T. C. Coleman, C. A. Mitchell, J. W. Graham, William Lee Alexander, and E. G. Morrow. Of these three, Spruill, Alexander, and Morrow were slain. The total contributions of the faculty past and present, of the University of North Carolina to the Confederate army was fourteen, of whom seven, or fifty per cent. were killed.

When we come to the records of the alumni themselves we shall find that heroic enthusiasm, which had been shown by the members of the faculty, the resident students and the villagers, also characterized to the highest degree the conduct of the alumni. The first deaths were not in battle, but from disease contracted in the service. The first victim of disease was probably John H. Fitts, of Warrenton, who died in June, 1861. But with the first great battle of the war, the University received her baptism of blood. At First Manassas she lost at least four of her alumni. And the first student of this University who had attained the rank of a commissioned officer in the Confederate army, and possibly the first of all, officer or private, to fall in battle was, William Preston Mangum. His father, the Hon. Willie P. Mangum, had clung to the Union which he had served so long and so well while there was hope, but when hope failed, he gladly gave the hope of his house to the Confederacy. The son enlisted in the Flat River Guards, afterwards company B, 6th North Carolina, and was made second lieutenant. A few days before the battle of First Manassas, the 6th was ordered to Winchester and from there was rushed forward to reinforce Beauregard at Manassas. They arrived on the field at the crisis of the conflict on the 21st. Col. Fisher, from want of experience, had failed to throw out skirmishers or to form a line of battle, and when the regiment emerged, moving in column from a low scattered wood, Rickett's section of the Sherman battery was seen directly in its front and within seventy-five yards of the head of the column. These guns were then firing on other troops and could not be turned immediately on the 6th. Two or three companies formed into line and delivered a volley which disabled the battery. The companies charged, and the guns were captured. Lieutenant Mangum was seen standing by one of the captured cannon, and while the firing was still fierce, was mortally wounded within an hour of the time he was first under fire. Three others of the students, Adolph Lastrapes and Mitchell S. Prudhomme, of Louisiana, and John H. Stone of Alabama, stand with Lieutenant Mangum at the head of that long list of alumni of this Institution who poured out their blood on the battle-fields from First Manassas to Appomattox.

I shall now give a few statistics of the alumni. Were our University records more complete, we should no doubt find that in some instances the figures which I shall give, would be raised much higher. The record of the 4th North Carolina was very brilliant at Fair Oaks or Seven Pines. It carried 678 men into action, and lost 77 killed and 286 wounded, with six missing, or 54 per cent of the total number carried into battle. The colonel of the 4th at Fair Oaks, and the acting brigade commander, was George Burgwyn Anderson, who had been a student of this University. He had seen service in the West before the war, and was one of the old officers then in the service of the United States, who offered his sword to his native State. He handled the brigade with such success and skill on this occasion, that it brought him a brigadier's commission within a fortnight. The 4th had other University men among its leaders: Bryan Grimes was its third colonel; Captain John B. Andrews of Company C., David M. Carter of Company E., and Jesse S. Barnes and John W. Dunham of Company F., were all University men and were conspicuous for their bravery, two of them falling in battle.

The University of North Carolina lost five of her sons at Shiloh, fuller records would probably double the number; she lost fourteen at Malvern Hill; nine at Sharpsburg, including Anderson and Branch who had both attained the rank of Brigadier. At Fredericksburg the University lost eight, and five at Chancellorsville.

In the Gettysburg campaign, the highwater mark of the Confederacy, the University lost 21. It is particularly to our credit to know that the regiment which sustained the heaviest loss of any regiment on either side in a single battle during the war, was under the command of a University man. The 26th North Carolina, had Zebulon B. Vance as its first colonel. He served until his election as governor in August, 1862. He was succeeded by Harry King Burgywn, said to have been at the time of his election, the youngest colonel in the Confederate Army, and not yet twenty-one years of age. The regiment was a part of Pettigrew's brigade. It will be more interesting to give its history in the words of Col. William F. Fox, a Federal officer, whose account may be taken as entirely without prejudice. He says in his work, *Regimental Losses in the Civil War*, (pages 555–556):

"At Gettysburg, the 26th North Carolina of Pettigrew's Brigade, Heth's Division, went into action with an effective strength which is stated in the regimental official report, as over 800 men" [820]. "They sustained a loss, according to Surgeon General Guild's report, of 86 killed and 502 wounded; * total, 588. In addition there were about 120 missing, nearly all of whom must have been wounded or killed;

---

* Under Lee's order of May 14, 1863, this included only those who were pronounced by the surgeons as unfit for duty.

but, as they fell into the enemy's hands, they were not included in the hospital report. This loss occurred mostly in the first day's fight, where the regiment encountered the 151st Pennsylvania * and Cooper's Battery of Rowley's Brigade, Doubleday's Division. The quartermaster of the 26th who made the official report on July 4th, states that there were only 216 left for duty after the fight on the 1st inst. The regiment then participated in Pickett's charge on the third day of the battle, in which it attacked the position held by Smyth's Brigade, Hoyt's Division, Second Corps. On the following day it mustered only 80 men for duty, the missing ones having fallen in the final and unsuccessful charge. In the battle of the first day, Captain Tuttle's company, [F.] went into action with three officers and eighty-four men; all of the officers and eighty-three of the men were killed or wounded. On the same day, and in the same brigade, (Pettigrew's), company C, of the 11th North Carolina lost two officers killed, and 34 out of 38 men, killed or wounded; Captain Bird, of this company, with the four remaining men, participated in the charge on the third of July, and of these the flag-bearer was shot, and the captain brought out the flag himself. This loss of the 26th North Carolina at Gettysburg, was the severest regimental loss during the war.'' The total loss of the regiment on the first day alone, based on the figures of Col. Fox, was in killed, wounded and missing, eighty-six and three-tenths per cent.† This loss exceeded by four per cent. the loss of the 1st Minnesota at Gettysburg, which amounted to eighty-two per cent. The 141st Pennsylvania comes second, with seventy-five and seven-tenths per cent. In the Franco-Prussian war, the heaviest loss was forty-nine per cent, sustained by the 16th German Infantry (3rd Westphalian) at Mars-la-Tour. In the charge of the Light Brigade, the loss was but thirty-six and seven-tenths per cent. Oh that the 26th North Carolina had a Tennyson to sing of its charge when no one had blundered ! But this same brigade of Pettigrew, shattered as it was by the three days fighting, was one of

---

* This regiment lost 335 men in killed, wounded and missing, on July 1.

† In *killed and wounded* alone, according to Colonel Fox, the 26th North Carolina stands third on the list of great losses, having seventy-one and seven-tenths per cent, against eighty-two and three-tenths per cent of the 1st Texas at Sharpsburg, and seventy-six per cent of the 21st Georgia at Manassas. That few of the "120 missing" from this regiment, on July 1, returned, is indicated by the number reported for duty on the 4th.

~~out of 820 men, or ninety-seven and five-tenths per cent.~~

2

the two to whom was given the post of honor in defending the rear
of the army of Northern Virginia on its retreat from Pennsylvania,
and it was on this retreat that the gallant Pettigrew was called to surrender his valuable life. Can this University desire more in the line
of military distinction, than to have the distinguished honor of claim-
ing Burgwyn and Pettigrew among her sons?

The following figures from Colonel Fox, give the absolute losses
of the twenty-seven Confederate regiments that suffered most at
Gettysburg:

Regiment	Brigade.	Division.	Killed.	Wounded.	Missing.	Total.
26th N. C	Pettigrew's..........	Heth's......	86	502	120	708
42d Miss......	Davis'.............	Heth's......	60	205	....	265
2d Miss.	Davis'....	Heth's......	49	183	....	232
11th N. C.....	Pettigrew's.	Heth's......	50	159	.....	209
45th N. C.....	Daniel's...........	Rodes'......	46	173	.....	219
17th Miss....	Barksdale's.........	McLaws'....	40	160	....	200
14th S. C....	Gregg's...........	Pender's....	26	220	6	252
11th Miss......	Davis'	Heth's...	32	170	....	202
55th N. C....	Davis'....	Heth's......	39	159	.....	198
11th Ga.	G. T. Anderson's....	Hood's.....	32	162	.....	194
38th Va.	Armistead's	Pickett's....	23	147	... .	170
6th N. C.....	Hoke's.	Early's......	20	131	21	172
13th Miss.....	Barksdale's.........	McLaws'....	28	137	.....	165
8th Ala	Wilcox's	Anderson's.	22	139	.....	161
47th N. C.....	Pettigrew's..........	Heth's.	21	140	.....	161
3d N. C . ..	Stewart's............	Johnson's...	29	127	.....'	156
2d N. C. Bat.	Daniel's............	Rodes'	29	124	.....	153
2d S. C	Kershaw's......... ..	McLaws'....	27	125	2	154
52d N. C	Pettigrew's........	Heth's......	33	114	....	147
5th N. C....	Iverson's............	Rodes'	31	112	.....|	143
32d N. C	Daniel's..	Heth's......	26	116	... .	142
43d N. C	Daniel's..	Heth's......	21	126	.....	147
9th Ga. .	G. T. Anderson's ...	Hood's	28	115	.....	143
1st Md. Bat..|	Stewart's...........	Johnson's...	25	119	....	144
3d Ark.	Robertson's	Hood's.....	26	116	,.....	142
23d N. C	Iverson's............	Rodes'......	41	93	... .	134
57th Va	Armistead's	Pickett's....	35	105	4	144

I must not fail to mention in this connection the record of Company C, 11th North Carolina, which was with Pettigrew at Gettysburg on July 1, and lost a captain and lieutenant, and thirty-four out
of thirty-eight men. The company had three separate captains on
that terrible day. The first was made major; the second, Thomas
Watson Cooper, class of 1860, was killed; the third, Edward R. Out-

law, freshman 1859–60, was promoted from lieutenant. Hoke's North Carolina brigade was not less distinguished for bravery than those already mentioned; with a single Louisiana brigade as support, it charged across the field on the third day, drove back the enemy, captured 100 prisoners and four flags. The brigade was commanded in its charge by Isaac E. Avery, colonel of the 6th North Carolina, who had been a student here 1847–48. He was wounded in the charge, and lived only long enough to write on an envelope crimson with his blood: "Major Tate, tell my father I died with my face to the foe."

Need we be surprised that with such examples of heroism as these, the death-roll of this University in the Gettysburg campaign foots up a score? Gen. James Johnston Pettigrew, Col. Harry King Burgwyn, Col. Isaac Erwin Avery, Lieut.-Col. Maurice Thompson Smith, Maj. Owen Neil Brown, Maj. George McIntosh Clark, Capt. Elijah Graham Morrow, Capt. Nicholas Collin Hughes, Capt. Thomas Watson Cooper, Capt. George Thomas Baskerville, Capt. Joel Clifton Blake, Capt. Thomas Oliver Closs, Capt. Edward Fletcher Satterfield, Capt. Samuel Wiley Gray, Lieut. Wesley Lewis Battle, Lieut. William Henry Gibson, Lieut. John Henderson McDade, Lieut. Richardson Mallett, Lieut. Jesse H. Person, Lieut. Iowa Michigan Royster, Lieut. William Henry Graham Webb.

At Vicksburg the University lost four; at Chickamauga seven; at the Wilderness six; at Spotsylvania Courthouse five, including Thomas M. Garrett whose commission as Brigadier-General arrived the day after his death. In the Atlanta campaign she lost nine; including Lieutenant-General Polk. At Bentonsville, the last battle in North Carolina, and the last struggle of Johnston's army, Lt.-Col. John D. Taylor, class of 1853, carried the first North Carolina battalion into battle with 267 men. He lost 152 men, or fifty-seven per cent. Lt.-Col. Taylor lost an arm, and Lieut.-Col. Edward Mallett, who commanded a regiment, lost his life. Capt. John H. D. Fain, the only child of his mother, fell on the last day of the last fight before Petersburg, April 2, 1865; Felix Tankersley was killed within three days of Lee's surrender; and James J. Phillips died from the effects of wounds received after Lee's surrender, but before the news had reached his cavalry commander. From First Manassas to Appomattox, the University saw the life blood of her alumni poured out in lavish profusion. From Gettysburg to Missouri and Texas; on every important battlefield of the war, by death in battle, by death from wounds, by disease and as prisoners of war, did the sons of this University manifest their devotion to the cause. The University of North Carolina saw its alumni occupying positions in the Confederate army from private to Lieutenant-General, and it made its offerings on the altar of the grim god of war from every rank with the sole exception of major-general, and she was not less liberal with the highest in rank than with the lowest. Of the Confederate officers highest in rank who were slain in battle, one had attained the rank of general; three were lieutenant-generals and here again, the University was called on to give more than her share to the sacrifice, in the person of Leonidas Polk. She lost besides, Lieutenant-General Polk, four Brigadier-Generals, Anderson, Branch, Garrott and Pettigrew, eleven colonels, nine lieutenant-colonels and eight majors.

This University claims further, more than her proportion of the commanders of North Carolina regiments that became distinguished because of their heavy losses in individual battles. There are nine regiments of which we have records of the numbers carried into battle, and the losses sustained in each. Thus the 33rd North Carolina, under the command of C. M. Avery, met with a loss of forty-one and four-tenths per cent at Chancellorsville; the 3d North Carolina lost fifty per cent at Gettysburg; the 4th North Carolina under G. B. Anderson, fifty-four and four-tenths per cent at Seven Pines; the 7th North Carolina, fifty-six and two-tenths per cent at Seven Days; the 18th, under R. H. Cowan, fifty-six and five-tenths per cent at Seven Days; the 1st North Carolina battalion, under John D. Taylor, fifty seven per cent at Bentonsville; the 27th North Carolina, sixty-one and two-tenths per cent at Sharpsburg; the 2nd North Carolina battalion, sixty-three and seven-tenths per cent at Gettysburg; the 26th North Carolina, under H. K. Burgwyn, eighty-six and three-tenths per cent at Gettysburg. It will be seen that four of the nine regiments were under command of University men at the time of meeting their heaviest loss.

The following list of North Carolina regiments suffering heavy losses is extracted from Colonel Fox's book. It is given for general information and for the reason that about one-half of these regiments at the time of sustaining their losses had University men as colonels or lieutenant-colonels [viz: 33, 26, 21, 4, 23, 35, 49 (Major), 18, 48, 13, 6, 49, 57, 48 (Major), 18, 13, 17, 4, 33, 23, 18, 26, 11, 45, 55, 6, 5, 43, 23]:

Regiment.	Battle.	Killed.	Wounded.	Missing.	Total.	Rank in Numbers Lost.
33d N. C.	Newbern	32	28	144	204	1
26th "	"	5	10	72	87	2
21st "	Front Royal	21	59	..	80	1
4th "	Fair Oaks, May 31–June 1, 62	77	286	6	369	1
23d "	" " "	18	145	6	169	2
48th "	Oak Grove, June 25	18	70	....	88	...
1st "	Mechanicsville	36	105	1	142	2
20th "	Gaines' Mill	70	202	.....	272	....
15th "	Malvern Hill	21	110	.....	131	...
25th "	"	22	106	5	133	....
35th "	"	18	91	18	127	....
49th "	"	14	75	16	105	...
7th "	Seven Days	35	218	......	253	1
18th "	"	45	179	......	224	2
12th "	"	51	160	1	212	3
28th "	"	19	130	....	149	....
37th "	"	27	111	......	138	....
15th "	Crampton's Gap, Md	11	48	124	183	....
3d "	Sharpsburg	46	207	....	253	1
48th "	"	31	186	.....	217	3
27th "	"	31	168	......	199	4
13th "	"	41	149	......	190	5
1st "	"	18	142	.....	160	..
15th "	"	16	143	....	159	....
6th "	"	10	115	....	125	....
49th "	"	16	61	......	77	...
57th "	Fredericksburg	32	192	......	224	1
48th "	"	17	161	......	178	2
15th "	"	10	93	.....	103	...
37th "	"	17	76	....	93	...
18th "	"	13	77	......	90	....
25th "	"	13	75	.....	88	....
7th "	"	5	81	......	86	....
28th "	"	16	49	......	65	....
16th "	"	6	48	......	54	....
37th "	Chancellorsville	34	193	......	227	1
2d "	"	47	167	......	214	2
13th "	"	31	178	7	216	3
3d "	"	38	141	17	126	4
22d "	"	30	139	15	184	5
17th "	"	37	127	...	164	6
4th "	"	45	110	58	213	7
33d "	"	32	101	66	199	....
23d "	"	32	113	35	180	....
1st "	"	34	83	27	144	....
18th "	"	30	96	.....	126	....
34th "	"	18	110	20	148	..
14th "	"	15	116	......	131	....
30th "	"	25	98	1	124	....

Regiment.	BATTLE.	Killed.	Wounded.	Missing.	Total.	Rank in Numbers Lost.
26th N. C....	Gettysburg	86	502	120	708	1
11th "	"	50	159	......	209	4
45th "	"	46	173	......	219	5
55th "	"	39	159	......	198	....
6th "	"	20	131	21	172	....
47th "	"	21	140	......	161	....
3d "	"	29	127	.....	156	....
2d " Bat...	"	29	124	....	153	....
52d " Regt..	"	33	114	.....	147	....
5th "	"	31	112	.....	143	....
32d "	"	26	116	.....	142	....
43d "	"	21	126	.....	147	....
23d "	"	41	93	......	134	..
51st "	Fort Wagner	16	52	.....	68	....
51st "	Charleston Harbor.........	17	60	......	77	1
8th "	"	4	43	......	47	....
31st "	"	13	32	....	45	.....

It has been ascertained that 312 of the students and graduates of this University lost their lives in the Confederate service. Taking the membership of the Dialectic and Philanthropic societies as representing the total matriculation in the University for any given period, it will be found that there were matriculated in the University in the forty-three years, 1825 to 1867 inclusive,* just 2929 persons. Out of these we know that 190, at least, had died before the war began. This will leave 2739 possible living alumni, (matriculates and graduates), of the Institution. Out of this number, 2729, we know that 312, or 11.39 per cent, lost their lives in the Confederate service.

It will perhaps never be accurately known how many saw service. Of the 2739 matriculates mentioned above as probably alive in 1861, we know that 1078, or 39.35 per cent. of the total enrollment of the University for the forty-three years, 1825–1867, were in the Confederate army.

If we examine the records for the ten years just before the war, we shall find that there were 1331 matriculates between 1851 and 1860 inclusive; that out of these 1331 at least 759 or fifty-six and two-

---

* This date has been taken because a number of ex-soldiers pursued studies in the University after the war was over.

tenths per cent. saw service in the Confederate States army, and they were in all grades from private to brigadier-general. Of the 759 that we know, 234 were killed. This means that thirty per cent. of those who went into the Confederate service from the University of North Carolina for those ten years, sealed their faith with their blood. This death rate is very near the average of the per cent. of loss sustained by North Carolina troops as a whole, and represents seventeen and five-tenths per cent. of the total enrollment of the University for the ten years. In other words, the proportional loss sustained on the total enrollment of students for these ten years, was just about twice as great as that sustained by the Federal army. The rates of losses of that army, moreover, were greater than were those in the Crimean, or in the Franco-Prussian war. If we reduce this proportion to its proper basis of enlisted men, it will be found that the losses in the Federal army from all causes, death in battle, death from wounds, death by disease and in prison, was eight and six-tenths per cent.* Of the 1078 University men who are known to have served in the Confederate army, we know that 312, or 28.94 per cent lost their lives; more complete records of their service would no doubt reduce this per cent, but it is not probable that the most complete returns of the service of our students would reduce it to less than twenty-five per cent or three times as heavy as the losses sustained by the Federal army.

It will give us a clearer conception of the immense energy displayed by this University, to compare its losses with the losses of some other institutions. The University of Virginia Memorial gives the number of students of that institution who were killed, as 198. Professor Trent estimates that there were perhaps 300 killed in all, and that twenty-five per cent of its students saw service in the C. S. A. The number of students of the Virginia Military Institute reported as killed, was 171. I have found no figures for other Southern institutions. Of northern institutions we find that all contributed more or less of their graduates to the army of the Union. Lafayette College, Pennsylvania, had 226 students who served in that army. Of its regular graduates living, and not beyond the age for military service, twenty-six per cent were in the army. The average of ser-

---

* See Col. Fox's article in *The Century*, on the chance of being hit in battle. In his larger work, Regimental Losses, he says that the general Confederate loss in *killed and wounded*, was nearly ten per cent, while the Federal loss in killed and wounded, was nearly five per cent.

vice for the New England colleges, was 23 per cent; Yale leads the list with twenty-five per cent. Between 1825 and 1864, 1384 students received the degree of A. B. from the University of North Carolina; of these, we know that 537, or nearly forty per cent., were in the service of the Confederate States.

But this comparison is unjust to the University of North Carolina, for I have mentioned already the enthusiasm with which her students rushed away to battle without finishing their work. There were eighty members of the Freshman class of 1859–60. But a single one (Titus W. Carr), remained to complete his studies and he was rendered unfit for service by feeble health. The class of 1860 had eighty-four members; two of them died in 1860; of the remaining eighty-two, it seems from the best evidence at hand, that eighty entered the Confederate service; of these 80, 23, or 28.75 per cent were killed. There were few graduates the next year. Five members of the faculty had gone as we have already seen. The halls of the University which had presented such a scene of bustling activity a few years before, were now almost deserted. There was danger that the Institution would be compelled to close from the sheer lack of students.

Further, the enforcement of the conscription acts threatened to bring about the same result. The trustees then determined to appeal to President Davis in behalf of the institution and its students. Mr. Davis had said at the beginning of the war, that "the seed corn must not be ground up." At their meeting in Raleigh, October 8, 1863, the trustees resolved, "That the President of the University be authorized to correspond with the President of the Confederate States, asking a suspension of any order or regulation which may have been issued for the conscription of students of the University, untill the end of the present session, and also with a view to a general exemption of young men advanced in liberal studies, until they shall complete their college course.

"That the President of the University open correspondence with the heads of other literary institutions of the Confederacy, proposing the adoption of a general regulation, exempting for a limited time from military service, the members of the *two higher classes* of our colleges, to enable them to attain the degree of Bachelor of Arts."

In accord with these instructions, Gov. Swain addressed the following letter to President Davis:

UNIVERSITY OF NORTH CAROLINA,
CHAPEL HILL, N. C., *October 15, 1863.*

" *To his Excellency,* JEFFERSON DAVIS,
President of the Confederate States.

SIR—The accompaning resolutions, adopted by the trustees of this institution at their regular meeting in Raleigh, on the eighth instant, make it my duty to open a correspondence with you on the subject to which they relate.

A simple statement of the facts, which seem to me to be pertinent, without any attempt to illustrate and enforce them by argument, will, I suppose, sufficiently accomplish the purposes of the trustees.

At the close of the collegiate year 1859–60 (June 7th, 1860), the whole number of students in our catalogue was 430. Of these, 245 were from North Carolina, 29 from Tennessee, 28 from Louisiana, 28 from Mississippi, 26 from Alabama, 24 from South Carolina, 17 from Texas, 14 from Georgia, 5 from Virginia, 4 from Florida, 2 from Arkansas, 2 from Kentucky, 2 from Missouri, 2 from California, 1 from Iowa, 1 from New Mexico, 1 from Ohio. They were distributed in the four classes as follows: Seniors 84, Juniors 102, Sophomores 125, Freshmen 80.

Of the eight young men who received the first distinction in the Senior class, four are in the grave, and a fifth a wounded prisoner. More than a seventh of the aggregate number of graduates are known to have fallen in battle.

The Freshman class of eighty members pressed into service with such impetuosity, that but a single individual remained to graduate at the last commencement [Titus W. Carr]; and he in the intervening time had entered the army, been discharged on account of impaired health, and was permitted by special favor to rejoin his class.

The faculty at that time was composed of fourteen members, no one of whom was liable to conscription. Five of the fourteen were permitted by the trustees to volunteer. One of these has recently returned from a long imprisonment in Ohio, with a ruined constitution, [G. B. Johnston]. A second is a wounded prisoner, now at Baltimore. A third fell at Gettysburg, [I. M. Royster]. The remaining two are in active field service at present.

The nine gentlemen who now constitute the corps of instructors are, with a single exception, clergymen, or laymen beyond the age of conscription. No one of them has a son of the requisite age, who has not entered the service as a volunteer. Five of the eight sons of members of the faculty are now in active service; one fell mortally wounded at Gettysburg, [W. L. Battle]; another at South Mountain, [J. C. Battle].

The village of Chapel Hill owes its existence to the University, and is of course materially affected by the prosperity or decline of the institution. The young men of the village responded to the call of the country with the same alacrity which characterized the college classes; and fifteen of them—a larger proportion than is exhibited in any other town or village in the State—have already fallen in battle. The departed are more numerous than the survivors; and the melancholy fact is prominent with respect to both the village and the University, that the most promising young men have been the earliest victims.

Without entering into further details, permit me to assure you as the result of extensive and careful observation and inquiry, that I know of no similar institution or community in the Confederacy that has rendered greater services, or endured greater losses and privations, than the University of North Carolina, and the village of Chapel Hill.

The number of students at present here is 63; of whom 55 are from North Carolina, 4 from Virginia, 2 from South Carolina, and 1 from Alabama; 9 Seniors, 13 Juniors, 14 Sophomores, and 27 Freshmen.

A rigid enforcement of the conscription act may take from us nine or ten young men with physical constitutions in general, better suited to the quiet pursuits of literature and science than to military service. They can make no appreciable addition to the army; but their withdrawal may very seriously affect our organization, and in its ultimate effects cause us to close the doors of the oldest University at present accessible to the students of the Confederacy.

It can scarcely be necessary to intimate that with a slender endowment, and a diminution of more than $20,000 in annual receipts for tuition, it is at present very difficult, and may soon be impossible to sustain the institution. The exemption of professors from the operation of the conscript act is a sufficient indication that the annihilation of the best established colleges in the country, was not the purpose of our Congress; and I can but hope, with the eminent gentlemen who have made me their organ on this occasion, that it will never be permitted to produce effects which I am satisfied no one would more deeply deplore than yourself.

I have the honor to be, with the highest consideration, your obedient servant,

D. L. SWAIN.*

This appeal was not in vain. Orders were issued from the Conscript office to Captain Landis, the district enrolling officer, to grant the exemptions requested. Col. Peter Mallett, the commandant of conscripts, in communicating the information to Governor Swain says: "In performing this duty, Governor, I must express to you the great gratification and interest felt in perusing the report, which will be filed at this office with pride as a North Carolinian, as a relic rather than as a public document."

But this exemption did not relieve all the necessities of the Institution. On the 5th of March, 1864, the trustees instructed Governor Manly their secretary, to forward a second petition, praying for the exemption of the Freshman and Sophomore classes. It is as follows:

HON. JAMES A. SEDDON, Secretary of War.

The trustees of the University of North Carolina at a late meeting adopted the resolution, a copy of which is hereto attached, marked A, to which I beg leave to invite your attention.

By a report made to the Executive Committee of the trustees, Governor Swain, the President of the University—the composition of the four classes are as follows:

There are nine (9) members of the Senior Class; of these, two (2) have joined the army, two have substitutes, two have seen hard service in the army, one is under eighteen years of age and one permanently disabled.

Junior Class, consisting of fifteen members; of these, seven have substitutes, five have been in the army, two are under eighteen years of age, and one, F. R. Bryan, is dead. This class at the close of the Sophomore year numbered thirty, all of whom, except fifteen named above, are supposed to be in the army.

These two classes were heretofore, by your kind favor, granted permission to finish their collegiate course, which the Senior Class will have accomplished by the first Thursday in June next.

Sophomore Class. This class at the end of its Freshman year, numbered twenty-four; of these sixteen are supposed to have entered

---

* Printed in Mrs. Spencer's Last Ninety Days of the War in North Carolina, pages 257–260.

the army. Of the nine now remaining, three are exempt from physical disability, and one or more of these three left the class on that
account. In a communication by President Swain to Governor
Vance he says: " Our Sophomore Class is now reduced to six regular members. Morehead (who has a substitute, an Englishman over
conscript age) is the best, and Mickle, the second best scholar in it.
The latter has a slender constitution, and is in delicate health."

Freshman Class. Of the twenty-seven members of this class,
twenty-four are under age; and one over eighteen years of age,
Julius C. Mills of Caswell, who has a substitute. The remaining two
are Julius S. Barlow of Edgecombe, born January 5, 1845, and Isaac
R. Strayhorn of Orange, born August 7th, 1845.

I have been thus minute in relation to the Sophomore and Freshman Classes, for the reason that on them, the reliance for the contin-
uation of the exercises of the Institution must mainly depend. It
will be seen by reference to the numbers of the Sophomore and
Freshman classes and their ages, but few, very few soldiers can be
added to the army of the Confederacy, whilst the removal of that
small number may so reduce the classes as to render it necessary to
discontinue the exercises of the Institution, one of the oldest and
largest in the Confederacy; and disband the able and venerable corps
of instructors, some of whom have devoted their services to the
Institution for more than a quarter of a century, and others for nearly
a half century. To disband this able body in their declining years,
when their accustomed salaries are so necessary to their comfort in
the evening of life, would seem to be ingratitude. To continue
those salaries without corresponding service, would subject the trustees to merited censure.

And although the limited number instructed might not seem to
justify the salaries paid, yet when we consider that this Institution
numbered between four and five hundred students at the commencement of this war, by whom every state in the Confederacy was represented, it is most respectfully submitted whether the trustees are
not justified, even at the sacrifice of their scanty means, in using all
exertion to keep the Institution in its present condition of usefulness,
ready to meet the demands of the Confederacy when our independence shall be blessed with peace.

Pardon me sir, for suggesting in behalf of the trustees that your
aid in continuing these classes will greatly contribute to the contin-
uance of the Institution, whilst the army, to whose efficiency your
first duty is due, will not be materially affected.

Allow me to call to your attention, the letter written you by Governor Swain, on the 15th October, 1863, in which there are some interesting details connected with the University.

By order of the Board of Trustees.

CHAS. MANLY, *Secretary.*

To this request Mr. Seddon replied under date of March 10, 1864: "I cannot see in the grounds presented such peculiar or exceptional circumstances as will justify departure from the rules acted on in many similar instances. Youths under eighteen will be allowed to continue their studies, those over, capable of military service, will best discharge their duty and find their highest training in defending their country in the field."

When this decision became known at the University in the spring of 1864, the nine or ten students who were subject to conscription went into the army, and others went with them to share their fortunes. The catalogue shows but sixty matriculates for the whole scholastic year of 1863-64; the next was little better. The report of attendance, December 29, 1864, is interesting: Senior class, seven; Junior class, two; George Slover and J. T. Smith; first distinction to Smith, second to Slover. Sophomore class, twelve; of these, two absent from examination. Freshman class, nineteen. Even the catalogues are a silent witness of the intensity of the struggle. They are smaller, are on inferior paper, and have that oily look peculiar to Confederate imprints. The difficulties in the way of the faculty were many, but they struggled on. Dr. Charles Phillips rang the college bell with his own hands for the last six months, although there were hardly a dozen boys in the Institution. These, with two or three exceptions, were from the village. When the Federal army appeared, these two or three left the University, and walked to their homes in the neighboring counties, but the exercises went on, morning and evening prayers were attended as usual, even when Federal troops were on the campus.

Under these circumstances, few students had either the opportunity or desire to continue their course unbroken. Many began their studies before the war; a few of these came back, lame and halting, or perhaps with an arm or a leg missing. We find numerous records like these: William Harrison Craig, matriculated 1857, C. S. A., A. B. 1868; or like this, Walter Clark, Adj. C. S, A,. A. B. 1864,

Lieut.-Col. C. S. A.; or like Melvin E. Carter, Capt. C. S A., matriculated 1867.

The commencement of 1865 was the climax of sorrows. The Senior class on the first of June, consisted of fifteen members, but because of the exigencies of the country only William Curtis Prout was permitted to complete the course. Yet, because they accepted the invitation of the president to perform the usual exercises on commencement day, Edward G. Prout, Henry A. London and John R. D. Shepard were awarded A. B.; Junior class, o; Sophomore, 5; Freshman class, 2. There was not a single visitor from a distance to attend the commencement of 1865, save some thirty Federal soldiers, who had been detailed to remain and keep order. What a sad contrast was this to the brilliant commencement of 1859, which was graced by the presence of the President of the United States and of his Secretary of the Interior (Jacob Thompson), who was an alumnus of the University, with its graduating class of ninety-two members, the second largest in the history of the institution!

The last year of the war was not only a period of trial for the University, but for the village as well; for, being a University town, its main support then as now, was drawn directly or indirectly, from the University. When it declined, the village suffered in direct proportion. This difficulty was relieved to some extent by the arrival of refugees from other parts. Their coming created a demand for houses and gave some impetus to trade. Many of the young men had gone to the army, as we have seen. At first, whenever a few boys returned on furlough, parties, tableaux, dances, &c., were gotten up in their honor. But this stopped after Gettysburg. The cords of sorrow were being tightened around her. But its community brought all men closer together; charity was more freely distributed, and the pride of station was forgotten. The bands of common sympathy became stronger as the pangs of common sufferings became more intense. The hardness of life was little thought of then; rich and poor fared alike; for all comforts and most necessities went to the soldiers in the field. "When a whole village poured in and around one church building to hear the ministers of every denomination pray the parting prayers and invoke the farewell blessings in unison on the village boys, there was little room for sectarian feeling, Christians of every name drew nearer to each other. People who wept and prayed and rejoiced together as we did for four years, learned to love each other more. The higher and nobler and more generous impulses of our nature were brought constantly into action, stimulated by the heroic endurance and splendid gallantry of our soldiers." *

The village of Chapel Hill was taken possession of by Federal troops on April 17, 1865. The brigade was under the command of General S. D. Atkins, of Illinois, and was composed of 4,000 Michigan cavalry. He moved his division westward seventeen days later, except a single company, which occupied the college buildings for more than two months. During May General Couch passed through the village at the head of 12,000 men. It is worthy of note that the entire damage sustained by the village and college from the invaders is estimated by Governor Swain not to have exceeded $100. Nor was this occupation without a tinge of romance, for in the midst of these surroundings the daughter of Governor Swain was wooed and won by General Atkins, and Cupid began the work of Reconstruction.

The following summary of statistics of Confederate dead of the University of North Carolina is made up from the list prepared by Colonel William L. Saunders for the four tablets in Memorial Hall (which contain 271 names, and give rank and class), from the additions to the list found in the catalogue of the Dialectic Society (containing 308 names), edited by Dr. William J. Battle; from the additions found in the Register of the Philanthropic Society (containing 272 names), edited by the present writer; from the the " Biographical Sketches of the Confederate dead of the University of North Carolina" (containing 162 names), edited by the present writer and published in the *North Carolina University Magazine*, 1887–91, and from other miscellaneous sources, chiefly correspondence:

TOTAL NUMBER OF CONFEDERATE DEAD, 312.

By place of residence at time of matriculation in the University:

Arkansas,	-	-	-	1	Virginia, -	-	-	-	8
California,	-	-	-	1	Florida, -	-	-	-	9
Iowa,	-	-	-	1	Mississippi,	-	-	-	11
Missouri, -	-	-	-	1	Tennessee,	-	-	-	11
Texas,	-	-	-	4	Louisiana,	-	-	-	14
South Carolina,		-	-	5	Alabama, -	-	-	-	18
Georgia, -	-	-	-	7	North Carolina,		-	-	221

* Mrs. C. P. Spencer's correspondence with author and her Last Ninety Days of the War in North Carolina.

By Occupation:

Editors,	-	-	-	2	Teachers, -	-	-	-	14
Civil Engineers,		-	-	5	Farmers, -	-	-	-	27
Preachers,	-	-	-	8	Lawyers, -	-	-	-	62
Merchants,	-	-	-	8	No occupation or unknown,				173
Physicians,	-	-	-	13					

By Rank in Service:

Lieutenant-General,	-	-	1	Surgeons and assistants,		-	5
Brigadier-Generals,	-	-	4	Aides,	-	-	-	2
Colonels, -	-	-	-	12	Captains, -	-	-	-	67
Lieutenant-Colonels,		-	6	Lieutenants,	-	-	-	69
Majors,	-	-	-	17	Corporals and Sergeants,	-	23
Adjutants,	-	-	-	4	Privates, -	-	-	-	100
Sergeant-Majors,		-	-	2					

Form of Death.

Died of wounds (including all of those whose wounds proved almost immediately fatal), - - - 55	Died of disease and in prison, - - - - 97
	Killed in battle, - - 160

University Men in the Closing Days of the War.

In the closing days of the struggle, University men, as usual, came to the rescue of their suffering country and sought to lighten the burthen of its sorrows. From the time of the fall of Vicksburg and the defeat at Gettysburg, it became evident to thoughtful men that the main hope of the Confederacy lay in negotiation with the United States. In 1861 Governor Graham had advised that the State of North Carolina hold her destiny in her own hands, instead of surrendering it to others. Time had proved the value of his position, and he was now a leader in the movement that looked toward peace with the United States, but the legal power of ending the war had been put by the Confederate Constitution into the hands of the President. Governor Graham was not among the confidential friends of President Davis, but worked through others, and had in this way a hand in setting on foot the Hampton Roads Conference. He was not a member of this Conference, but was President *pro tem.* of the Confederate Senate during the absence of Mr. Hunter on that mission.

After the failure of the Conference Governor Graham gave notice in the Confederate Senate that he would soon introduce a resolution in favor of opening negotiations with the United States upon the basis of a return to the Union by the States of the Confederacy. But the notice was not favorably received, and the Confederacy went down to its doom. When the crash came he was the same calm, conservative statesman that he had ever been, and was chosen by Governor Vance to accompany Governor Swain as an ambassador of peace to meet the incoming army of General Sherman. They surrendered the city of Raleigh to him and secured from him a promise of protection, which promise was, as a rule, observed. It was also through their efforts on this mission that the University was protected from vandalism. Besides this mission Governor Swain was one of the North Carolinians who was invited to Washington by President Johnson in the spring of 1865, to consult on the ways of restoring the State to the Union. B. F. Moore (A. B., 1820) and Robert P. Dick (A. B., 1843) were also members of this committee.

It must be kept in mind also that the consent of the Federal administration to the Hampton Roads Conference, the last ray of hope of the Confederacy, had been brought about largely through the influence of Francis P. Blair, who had been a student here.* Perhaps no student of this University has had a more remarkable career. He was at first a free soiler; then a Republican. He was the one leader of the unconditional Union men in Missouri, and fused former Democrats and former Republicans into a single strong body of unconditional Union men. The governor of the State and both houses of the assembly were Southern in sentiment, but Blair organized the German companies, which had been known as Wide-awakes in the presidential campaign, into companies of home guards, drilled them, armed them as he found means, and with them began to dominate the State. It was largely due to the influence of the Home Guards that a majority of 80,000 was given for the Union in February, 1861.

---

* Other alumni cast their fortunes with the Union as follows: Prof. Benj. S. Hedrick differed so radically in his political views from the ruling element, and was so outspoken that public sentiment forced his dismission from the faculty as early as 1856; another member, Rev. Solomon Pool, escaped the same fortune, probably, by being more circumspect in his language; Junius B. Wheeler served as engineer, assistant professor at West Point, and brevet colonel; Edward Jones Mallett was paymaster-general, 1862–65; Willie P. Mangum, Jr., was consul and vice-consul general in China and Japan, 1861–1881.

3

This vote broke down the strength of the secessionists and virtually turned the State over to Blair and his Home Guards. There were 65,000 stand of arms in the Federal Arsenal in St. Louis. It was the purpose of the State authorities to seize these arms, but the organizations of Blair prevented. Finally Blair rebelled against the power of the State and under his advice the State troops of Missouri were captured on May 10, 1861, without waiting for the necessary orders from Washington. This put an end to Southern supremacy and saved Missouri and Kentucky to the Union. Blair, became a Major-General in the Union army and commanded the 17th corps on Sherman's march to the sea.

XI. University Men and Confederate Education.

Such was the position of the alumni of the University in the field and in the legislative and executive branches of the general government of the Confederacy. Their work for Confederate Education was not less noticeable. Archibald D. Murphey was the first man to agitate the question of public schools in North Carolina. Bartlett Yancey drew the bill under which the public schools were organized, and Calvin H. Wiley was the organizer. These were all University men. Wiley succeeded in giving to North Carolina the best public school system that there was in the South before the war. He was Superintendent of Public Instruction in North Carolina during the war, and through his efforts, with the assistance of Governor Vance, the public schools of the State were kept open during the whole of the momentous period. In his report to Governor Vance in 1863 he says: "It is a subject of devout gratitude to one to be able to announce that our common schools still live and are full of glorious promise. Through all this dark night of storm their cheerful radiance has been seen on every hill and in every valley of our dear old State; and while the whole continent reels with the shock of terrible and ruthless war, covering the face of nature with ruin and desolation, there are here scattered through the wilderness hundreds of humming hives where thousands of youthful minds are busily learning those peaceful arts which, under the blessing of God, are to preserve our civilization and to aid in perpetuating the liberty and independence for which this generation is manfully contending." In the same year (1863) fifty counties reported 35,495 pupils, and fifty-four counties received $240,685.38 for schools. It is probable that there were then not less than 50,000 children in the State attending school.

This beneficent system remained vigorous to the end. The public school was maintained in North Carolina throughout the war, except in those sections where the Federals had control, and Sherman's army on its entrance into Raleigh found Dr. Wiley at his desk receiving reports and tabulating statements on the condition of the schools.

The position of Dr. Wiley among Southern educators, generally, was not less distinguished. He was regarded by all as an honored and trusted leader.* Another alumnus, Colonel William Bingham, class of 1856, remained at the head of his private school for boys during the whole of the war period. The school was continued at Oaks, in Orange county, and ten miles from a railroad, until the winter of 1864–65, when it was removed to Mebane, N. C. It was then put under a military organization, it officers were commissioned by the State, and the cadets were exempted from duty until eighteen years of age. The difficulties were great, one of the most serious being the lack of the necessary books. This want was met by the preparation of Bingham's series of English and Latin text-books, which have been republished since the war and are now used in every State of the Union.†

Perhaps the most curious of the educational enterprises of our alumni was the law school for Confederate prisoners, established on Johnson's Island in 1863 and 1864, by Joseph J. Davis (1847–50), who was then a prisoner of war.

XII. Governor Vance and the Part of North Carolina in the War.

But it is not until we come to the actual administration of affairs in North Carolina that we find the most exalted position that was filled by a son of this University, for it was Zebulon B. Vance who earned for himself the distinguishing epithet of "the War Governor of the South." This proud title was well deserved and has been generally recognized throughout the Union. It was earned through the masterful ability displayed by Governor Vance in his administration of the economic resources of the State. It was by his instrumentality largely that the blockade trade, carried on through the

---

*See *Proceedings* of the Convention of Teachers of the Confederate States, at Columbia, S. C., April 28, 1863 (Macon, Ga., 1863,).

† Latin Grammar, Greensboro, 1863; Cæsar's Commentaries, Greensboro, 1864.

port of Wilmington during 1863–64, became for a considerable time the main support of the North Carolina troops, and through them of the Confederacy. Goods were purchased by the State abroad on warrants that were backed by 11,000 bales of cotton and 100,000 barrels of rosin. Among the imports intended for use of the army directly were 50,000 blankets; shoes and leather sufficient for 250,000 pairs; gray woollen cloth for 250,000 uniforms; 12,000 overcoats ready made; 2,000 Enfield rifles with 100 rounds of fixed ammunition; 100,000 pounds of bacon; 500 sacks of coffee for hospital use; $50,000 worth of medicines at gold prices; large quantities of lubricating oils and other minor supplies of various kinds for the charitable institutions of the State, besides many other necessities of life needed by the people for every day use. The supplies of shoes, blankets, and clothing were more than enough for the North Carolina troops, and large quantities were turned over to the Confederate Government for the troops of other States. In the winter of 1863–64 Governor Vance supplied Longstreet's corps with 14,000 suits of clothing complete, and after the surrender of Joe Johnston, North Carolina had ready-made and in cloth 92,000 suits of uniform; there was also a great store of blankets, leather, &c. When Johnston's army surrendered it had five month's supplies for 60,000 men, and for many months Lee's army had drawn its supplies from North Carolina. It has been said that at the end of the war North Carolina had supplies sufficient for her to have still prolonged the struggle for two years. It was due to the executive ability of Governor Vance, a son of this University, that North Carolina found herself in this enviable position, and to this is due the fact that our people suffered less than other States, comparatively.

Not only did Governor Vance provide thoroughly for the wants of the soldiers in the field, but he was careful also to see that the families of the men in the army were not allowed to suffer. Granaries were established at certain points in the State, and corn was distributed to the most needy districts; commissioners were appointed in each county to look after the needy, and in this way the State became, for the time, a great almoner. Commissioners were appointed, whose sole duty was to provide salt, and the chief of the bureau for making salt, saltpeter, copperas, sulphur, sulphuric acids, and medical extracts, was Prof. W. C. Kerr, class of 1850. As early as 1862 he had been chemist and superintendent to the Mecklenburg Salt Company, whose works were located at Mt. Pleasant, near Charleston, S. C. He had made such improvements in the manufacture that the cost for wood was reduced one-half and other expenses lessened. The University takes an honorable place also in the manufacture of iron, for the second largest iron-mill in the Confederacy was owned and controlled by Robert R. and John L. Bridgers, both alumni, the former being also a member of the Confederate Congress. There was danger of an iron famine in the Confederacy, and at the request of the government the Messrs. Bridgers purchased the High Shoals iron property in Lincoln, Gaston, and Cleveland counties, N. C., and rebuilt the furnaces, forges, rolling-mills, nail factories, and foundaries. The States of North and South Carolina became, to a large extent, dependent on these mills, and they did also much government work.

It was through such extraordinary measures as these that the necessities of life and the sinews of war were supplied to the people of North Carolina. This had a reflex action upon them, and kept up their interest and enthusiasm throughout the fearful struggle; their *esprit de corps* was little altered by the reverses of the battle-field. They had confidence in their government at home. The soldier in the field felt that his wife and children would not be allowed to suffer while his State was able to provide. This gave him renewed strength for battle and caused him to show that magnificent heroism which has been for a generation the wonder and the admiration of the world. But this is at best but only a partial reason for the tremendous weight thrown by North Carolina into the scale in behalf of the Confederacy. No one man is, perhaps, so much responsible for this period of the HEROIC as this son of our University, Zebulon Baird Vance. And never was there a greater *Landstrum*, a more universal *levé en masse* than was seen in this quiet, slow moving old State during those four tremendous years. The white population of North Carolina in 1860 was 629,942; her military population was 115,369, being the third in rank in this respect. Her proper proportion of troops according to population was about one-tenth. She furnished in reality about one-fifth of the troops of the Confederacy. On a conservative estimate she sent to the Confederate armies 125,000 men, or an average of about one soldier to each white family. She furnished 10,000 more troops than she had military population in 1860. More than one-fourth of the Confederates killed in battle were North Carolinians; nearly one-fourth of those who died of wounds were North Carolinians; one-third of those who died of disease were North Carolinians; two-sevenths of the total losses of the Confederacy were North Carolinians. She lost 40,275 men, or about thirty-two per cent. of her total enrollment of 125,000. She lost more than twice as many troops as any other State, and yet surrendered twice as many troops as any other State at Appomattox. Prominent always among these troops of North Carolina were the alumni of this University. It was one of her alumni, General Bryan Grimes, class of 1848, who commanded the rear guard of Lee's army on its retreat from Petersburg, and it was the division under his command that, on the morning of April 9, 1865, made the last charge on the Federal lines that was ever made by the Army of Northern Virginia.

XIII. Epilogue.

Saving always the fact that North Carolinians did not, as a rule, develop the peculiar class of talent and character most highly esteemed by the President of the Confederacy, it seems safe to say that no educational institution contributed more to the Confederacy in proportion to relative strength than did the University of North Carolina. Not that this institution was more disloyal to the Federal Government than others in the South; not that her alumni were more pre-eminently given over to the doctrine of secession than were the alumni of other institutions; but when North Carolina saw, in May, 1861, that she had the choice between two evils and that she could not remain neutral in the pending struggle, she made the choice that was the most natural and reasonable. She chose the side of the State, or of local government, against the growing tendency toward centralization then given a new impetus by the Federal authorities. The alumni of her University responded gladly to her call to duty. They were faithful to the earlier teachings of their *Alma Mater.* They risked name and fame, life and fortune, for their State. They laid down their lives at her command.

The names of our Confederate dead are carved in marble on our memorial walls, but they have built themselves a monument more durable than marble. Their names are written in lines of living light

"On Fame's Eternal camping-ground."

The story of their heroism and their devotion to the call of duty wil be cherished by this University as the brightest jewel in her centennial crown, and their names will be remembered in this institution as long as patriotism is honored here, for

" where great deeds were done,
A power abides transfused from sire to son."